BIKE
ON,
BEAR!

For Clara. Believe in yourself, and when you don't think you can,
surround yourself with people who do —Cynthea Liu

To Matt—Kristyna Litten

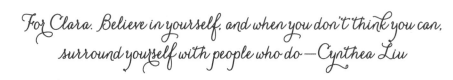

ALADDIN

An imprint of Simon & Schuster Children's Publishing Division
1230 Avenue of the Americas, New York, New York 10020
First Aladdin hardcover edition June 2015
Text copyright © 2015 by Cynthea Liu
Illustrations copyright © 2015 by Kristyna Litten

ALADDIN is a trademark of Simon & Schuster, Inc.,
and related logo is a registered trademark of Simon & Schuster, Inc.
For information about special discounts for bulk purchases, please contact Simon &
Schuster Special Sales at 1-866-506-1949 or business@simonandschuster.com.
The Simon & Schuster Speakers Bureau can bring authors to your live event.
For more information or to book an event contact the Simon & Schuster
Speakers Bureau at 1-866-248-3049 or visit our website at www.simonspeakers.com.
Designed by Jessica Handelman

The illustrations for this book were rendered in pencil, crayon, and digitally.
The text of this book was set in Bembo Infant.
Manufactured in China 0315 SCP
10 9 8 7 6 5 4 3 2 1
Library of Congress Cataloging-in-Publication Data
Liu, Cynthea.
Bike on, Bear! / by Cynthea Liu ; illustrated by Kristyna Litten. —
First Aladdin hardcover edition. pages cm
Summary: "Bear is an extraordinary, genius bear, who can do anything except ride
a bike. Can Bear figure out how to get on two wheels?" — Provided by publisher.
[1. Bears—Fiction. 2. Bicycles and bicycling—Fiction. 3. Determination(Personality trait)—
Fiction.] I. Litten, Kristyna, illustrator. II. Title.   PZ7.L739325Bik 2015
[E]—dc23 2014040726
ISBN 978-1-4814-0506-5 (hc)
ISBN 978-1-4814-0507-2 (eBook)

BIKE ON, BEAR!

By Cynthea Liu

Illustrated by Kristyna Litten

ALADDIN

New York · London · Toronto · Sydney · New Delhi

Bear was no ordinary cub.

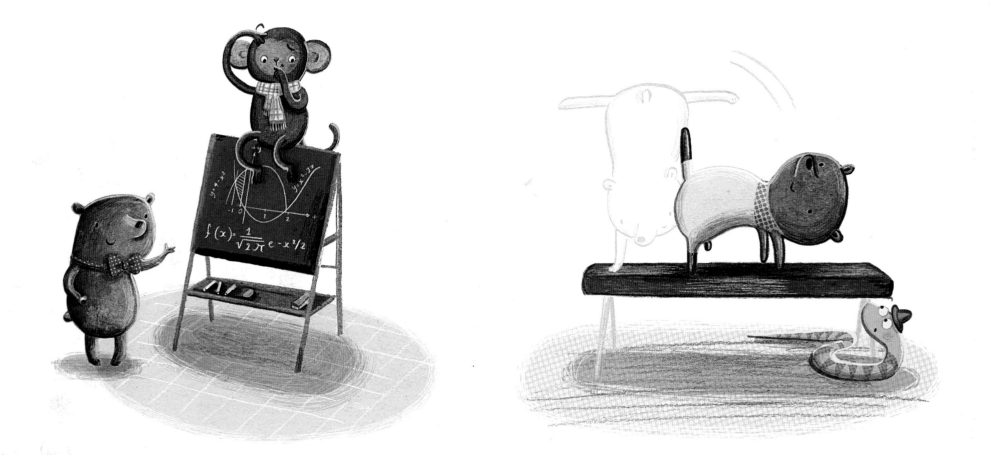

He was brainier
than a monkey . . .

More flexible than
a python . . .

And more helpful than
a brigade of beavers.

But Bear had a
very hairy problem.
He couldn't ride a bike.

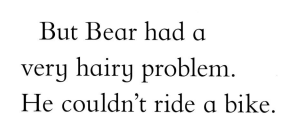

Not even with training wheels.

CRASH!

Not even with Daddy pushing him along.
"I'm going to let go now. Ready?"

CRASH!

Not even with ten of his best friends helping.
"Pedal, Bear. *Pedal!*"
"Brakes, Bear. *Brakes!*"

CRASH!

The situation was unbearable.

Then it got worse.

A brand-new park opened.
Bear read the sign.

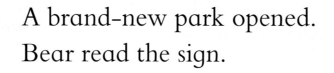

FLY YOUR KITES
PICNIC IN THE PARK
RIDE YOUR BIKES ON OUR BIKE PATH
(NO TRAINING WHEELS ALLOWED)

"Bike path?" said his friends. *"All right!"*
Bear gulped.

Bear was desperate. He wanted to ride with his buddies.
His mother gave him a big bear hug. "Try the library, dear,"
she suggested. "You can learn anything there."

EUREKA!

LEARN
TO RIDE A
BIKE
IN
④
DAYS

DAY
① *Get to know your bike.*

DAY
② *Practice your balance.*

DAY
③ *Believe in yourself.*

DAY
④ *Don't think about it too much!*

CHECK!

On day one, Bear studied his bike from end to end.

CHECK!

CHECK!

Bell

DING!

Diagram 1

Next, he ran some scientific calculations.

Bear was ready. He got on.

WHAP!

He fell over.

"Maybe you'll get it next time, buddy."

That evening, Bear went to a science fair.
While he presented his project, he wondered
what had gone wrong with the bike that day.
Hadn't he studied every part? Analyzed everything?

Was he just not smart enough?

On day two, Bear practiced his balance. He carefully placed a glass of water on his head and got on the bike. He put one foot on the pedal . . . and then the other.

He fell over. SPLASH! Bear *grrrrrred.*

"Just keep trying, champ."

That evening, Bear went to a gymnastics meet.
As he tiptoed across the beam, he wondered what
had gone wrong with the bike this time.
Why was balancing so hard?

clap

CLAP

clap

CLAP

Bear did a backward pike somersault.
The crowd cheered.

CLAP

On day three, Bear believed in himself.
"I can do this," he said.
He imagined himself riding a bike.
He stuck notes to his bathroom mirror.
He even dressed for the part.

He got on his bike and . . .
he fell over.

RIP!

He jumped on and blasted off.

And most importantly, he didn't think about it too much.

Bear tiptoed onto the seat, launched into a triple back-paw-spring, and nabbed the kid.

"Hooray, Bear!
That was some riding!"
Bear blushed.

Bear was no ordinary cub.

In fact, Bear could do practically anything.
"Bike on, Bear!"

MY HERO!

YOU'RE ACE, BEAR!

Bear ran some calculations. *Distance, height, wind speed.*
There wasn't much time!
He spotted a bike nearby.

Wheels, check! Handlebars, check! Brakes, check! Ding!

The next day, Bear trudged toward the library to return the book.
Suddenly, someone shouted from the park.

That evening, Bear didn't believe in himself *at all*.

His science project exploded.

His triple back-paw-spring
was a disaster.

And he couldn't even help out a fellow bear.
"I don't know how to put it back together, guys. I give up!"

Except maybe . . .